W9-DCI-149

SECRETS OF AN OVERWORLD SURVIVOR

WHEN LAVA STRIKES

SECRETS OF AN OVERWORLD SURVIVOR
WHEN LAVA STRIKES

GREYSON MANN

ILLUSTRATED BY GRACE SANDFORD

Sky Pony Press
New York

This book is not authorized or sponsored by Microsoft Corp., Mojang AB, Notch Development AB or Scholastic Inc., or any other person or entity owning or controlling rights in the Minecraft name, trademark, or copyrights.

Copyright © 2017 by Hollan Publishing, Inc.

Minecraft® is a registered trademark of Notch Development AB.

The Minecraft game is copyright © Mojang AB.

This book is not authorized or sponsored by Microsoft Corp., Mojang AB, Notch Development AB or Scholastic Inc., or any other person or entity owning or controlling rights in the Minecraft name, trademark, or copyrights.

All rights reserved. No part of this book may be reproduced in any manner without the express written consent of the publisher, except in the case of brief excerpts in critical reviews or articles. All inquiries should be addressed to Sky Pony Press, 307 West 36th Street, 11th Floor, New York, NY 10018.

Sky Pony Press books may be purchased in bulk at special discounts for sales promotion, corporate gifts, fund-raising, or educational purposes. Special editions can also be created to specifications. For details, contact the Special Sales Department, Sky Pony Press, 307 West 36th Street, 11th Floor, New York, NY 10018 or info@skyhorsepublishing.com.

Sky Pony® is a registered trademark of Skyhorse Publishing, Inc.®, a Delaware corporation.

Minecraft® is a registered trademark of Notch Development AB.
The Minecraft game is copyright © Mojang AB.

Visit our website at www.skyponypress.com.

10 9 8 7 6 5 4 3 2 1

Library of Congress Cataloging-in-Publication Data is available on file.

Special thanks to Erin L. Falligant.

Cover illustration by Grace Sandford
Cover design by Brian Peterson

Hardcover ISBN: 978-1-5107-1328-4
Ebook ISBN: 978-1-5107-1329-1

Printed in the United States of America

Interior design by Joshua Barnaby

SECRETS OF AN OVERWORLD SURVIVOR

WHEN LAVA STRIKES

CHAPTER 1

Will zoomed down the dark tunnel in his minecart, leaning from side to side as the tracks jogged left, then right. He braced himself as the cart climbed upward, slowing to a crawl. It teetered at the top of the tracks and then—

"Will, watch out!"

Mina's warning jolted Will out of his daydream. He glanced down, realizing he was about to topple into a deep ravine. *Yikes!* He jumped backward, gripping the branch of a spruce tree for support.

"You're moving too fast!" cried Mina, her hand on her heart. "We're in the extreme hills now. You have to watch for drop-offs, ravines, even streams of hot lava. That's why we left Shadow at your house, remember?"

Will's cheeks burned with embarrassment. "I know," he snapped. "I'm fine." But as the wind whipped through his hair, he glanced back down at the steep ravine and shuddered. *That was a close call.*

"What were you daydreaming about, anyway?" asked Mina as they picked their way carefully along the path. "Were you thinking about Shadow?"

Will shook his head. Sure, he missed the yellow tabby cat that he and Mina had found in the jungle. But he knew Shadow would be safest staying at home with his brother, Seth.

"No," he admitted, "I was actually imagining how much fun it'll be to find an abandoned mineshaft." He felt a rush of excitement just saying the words.

Mina hoisted up the pack on her back and nodded happily. "I know. The hills up here are *full* of treasures. I can't wait to—"

"—ride some minecarts!" interrupted Will.

"—mine some redstone!" finished Mina. "Wait, what? Minecarts? Sure, that'll be fun. But the caves around here have *real* treasure, Will. Like the redstone I need to make my potions last longer. And giant slimes, which drop slimeballs. I need those to make magma cream for my potion of fire resistance. And we might find gold and diamonds—even emeralds!"

Will shrugged. Right now, he wasn't thinking about all that stuff. Maybe he and Mina just disagreed about what *real* treasures were.

I know Mina's all about her potion ingredients, he thought as he followed her bobbing ponytail up the trail. *But why call this land the "extreme hills" if you can't have extreme adventures? And a little fun?*

"You know, Will," she called over her shoulder, "if we find diamonds, you could craft a diamond sword."

That stopped him in his tracks. Will glanced at the iron sword strapped to his side. It was strong and quick, for sure. But a diamond sword?

He could battle *any* mob with that—from zombies and spider jockeys to the Ender Dragon itself!

"Yeah," he said dreamily. "I guess a diamond sword *would* be cool." And with that, he was off in another daydream, battling a winged dragon with his sparkly new sword.

So when Mina stopped to enjoy the view ahead, Will *didn't* stop. He walked right past her. Right over the edge.

He felt the rocks slide out from beneath him, and then he was falling! Down, down, down . . .

Mina screamed from up above. Or was *he* the one screaming?

He scrunched his eyes shut, pulled himself into a tight little ball, and braced for impact.

CHAPTER 2

Splash!

The icy cold took Will's breath away. As he plunged deep into the dark pool of water, he opened his eyes. Which way was up? He searched for light but saw nothing.

Swim, he ordered his frozen limbs. And, with some effort, they did.

Finally his head broke the surface. He gasped for breath. He spun in a circle, treading water, trying to see through the darkness at the bottom of the ravine.

"Will!" Mina's voice rang out from above.

He glanced up and was relieved to spot her red-haired head dangling down toward him, a patch of blue sky behind her. But, boy, she was a long way up!

Don't panic, thought Will, trying to catch his breath.

"Are you okay?" Mina called down.

"I—I think so," he answered, his teeth chattering. His arms and legs felt stiff with cold. He had to get out of this cave pool before . . . well, before he *couldn't.*

Now that his eyes were getting used to the dark, Will could make out the edge of the pool. He paddled toward it and gripped the slippery rock, but he didn't have the strength to pull himself out.

My pack's too heavy! It felt like a thousand pounds. He struggled to slide his arms out of the straps, one by one. Then with a kick of his legs, he hoisted the pack up and onto the rock.

Finally, with every ounce of energy he could muster, he lodged his fingers into the crevices of the rock and pulled himself out, too.

"Will!"

Mina kept calling his name, but he was too tired to answer. Finally he rolled onto his back and gave her a shaky thumbs-up.

"I'm dropping down a rope!" she called. But as she snaked a knotted rope down into the ravine, Will heard the flutter of wings.

He sat up straight. A gazillion bats were waking up in the shadowy cave around him. All at once, they lifted off from every nook and cranny in one giant swarm. He ducked, his heart racing, and reached for his bow and arrow.

"Will, no!" Mina pleaded. "Don't hurt them! They're harmless."

"How do you know?" he asked, his voice coming out weak and wobbly.

"Because I've seen them before," said Mina. "They don't drop any potion ingredients either. They're as worthless as silverfish."

Silverfish? Will didn't know what those were. But as his eyes searched the corners of the cave, wondering where the bats had come from, he saw two gaping holes—no, three. Tunnel openings! Where did they lead?

"Can you reach the rope?" asked Mina.

Will didn't even look for it. "You should come down here instead," he called excitedly. "I see tunnels!"

Mina hesitated. "We don't know where they lead, Will. It's not safe. We should wait till we find a real mineshaft."

Will groaned. This wasn't the time to play it safe. This was the time for adventure! How could he convince Mina to come down?

He thought hard and then smiled into the darkness. "You know," he called to Mina, "I think there could be redstone down here. Yup, I think

I see some. And diamonds! And giant slimes—hey, there's one right now!"

Mina giggled. "There is not."

But it worked. She tied the rope to a tree and soon was climbing carefully down.

"Alright," she said, winding the rope back up. "We have to move *slowly* through the tunnels, Will. We have to watch for signs of danger."

"Like what?" he asked, wringing the water out of his clothes.

"Like the bubbling sound of hot lava. Or glowing drips of molten rock on the ceiling, which means that lava could flow down on us at any moment. We have to be very careful where we mine."

Will nodded as if he were listening, but really he was thinking about which tunnel to enter first. "This one," he said, pointing toward the largest opening.

"Why?" asked Mina.

Will shrugged. "I just have a feeling."

So Mina lit a torch and they started into the winding tunnel. Will fought the urge to run ahead. What would they find around the next bend?

"Slow down," Mina reminded him. Then she spotted something.

"Redstone! Good call on the tunnel, Will!" She crouched low and held out the torch to show him the flecks of red in the stone.

Mina pulled out her pickaxe and started hacking at the base of the wall. "Oh, this axe is getting so worn out," she cried in frustration, examining the pointed end. "Can you help?"

Will shrugged. He wasn't much of a miner, but Seth had made sure he brought a pickaxe this time. So he pulled it from his pack and started whacking at the wall next to Mina.

Small blocks of redstone piled up at her feet, and she quickly gathered them up. But hard as he tried, Will couldn't get his stone to break.

"What's up with this rock?" he said. "It's super hard."

"It is?" Mina looked over. She sucked in her breath before hollering, "Stop! It's a monster egg!"

Will heard the words just as he took his last whack at the rock. And as it exploded into shards, something popped out and scurried around his feet.

"Silverfish!" said Mina, clamping her hand over her mouth.

"Oh! So that's a silverfish," said Will, squatting to get a better look at the gray bug. "He seems harmless enough."

"Sure he is," whispered Mina. "But wait until he wakes up all his friends."

Will watched with horror as the rock wall crumbled. Silverfish tumbled out, climbing over one another and spilling onto the floor. Soon the scuttling, squeaking bugs surrounded him.

And then they began to attack.

CHAPTER 3

Will lashed out at the silverfish with his sword, again and again. But for every one he killed, more seemed to spill out of the walls!

"Get up here!" cried Mina, who had climbed onto a stone block.

Will jumped up beside her, teetering. He pictured himself toppling into the sea of silverfish. Would they eat him alive?

From the safety of the rock, he attacked the bugs. One, two, three . . . ten, twenty, thirty. Finally there was only one left. As the black-eyed bug scurried toward the rock, Mina struck it with her sword.

"Nasty, annoying little creatures," she muttered. "I *told* you they were worthless!" She shuddered and shook her arms and legs, as if the bugs were still attacking her.

Will couldn't agree more. But as he looked at the gaping hole the bugs had left in the wall, he saw something. Or rather, he saw *nothing*. The hole led straight through the wall to a giant, open cavern.

He stepped toward the hole and peeked through. "Um, the silverfish weren't totally worthless," he whispered to Mina.

"Huh?"

"Look what they found for us," he said, pointing. "An abandoned mineshaft!"

Mina knelt carefully beside him, and together, they peered over the edge.

The shaft was so deep, it made Will's head spin. A long ladder led straight down, past glowing torches and tunnel openings.

And the base camp below was bathed in soft light. It was a mineshaft, alright, but it didn't look abandoned.

"Should we go down?" he asked. But he was already reaching for the top rung of the ladder, lowering himself backward into the shaft.

"Okay," said Mina. "But be careful, Will. Sometimes miners set traps so that people don't loot their mines."

Traps? Will didn't see anything like that below. In fact, the miner's camp looked pretty inviting. He sped down the ladder, eager to reach the bottom.

Just before he hopped to the floor, Mina called out, "Stop!"

Will's foot froze only a few inches above the stone. "What?" he cried. "You almost gave me a heart attack!"

"Don't you see the trip wire?" she asked, pointing from overhead. "There are hooks on either side! See?"

Will glanced back down. He could barely make out a thin, white string in his path. And beyond it? A wooden trapdoor. Did the trip wire open the door? If it did, he might have fallen through that door into who knows where.

He took a deep breath and stepped sideways off the ladder, clearing the wire. *Mina was right,* Will thought with a sigh—which meant that now she'd be more cautious than ever.

As Mina pulled out a pair of scissors and carefully snipped the string, he scanned the mineshaft. Was the miner here somewhere? Suddenly this base camp seemed a lot less inviting.

"Hello?" he called out. His greeting bounced off the walls and came back to him like a boomerang. "Hello?"

Mina froze beside him, waiting for a response. After a moment, she whispered, "I don't think there's anyone here."

Will pointed upward. "But the torches are lit. See? Someone must have been here this morning."

Mina glanced up at the glowing lamps and shook her head. "Those are redstone torches. They can stay lit like that for forever."

Will shrugged and took a few steps into the mine. As he wandered past the bed, furnace, and crafting table, he wondered about the miner who had created this camp. Where was he now?

"Over here!" called Mina. "There's an old sack of potatoes. See the roots growing out of these? I really don't think anyone has been here for a while." She sounded relieved.

The potatoes *did* look old and wrinkly. Then Will saw the wooden chest beside the potatoes. "Is that what I think it is?" he asked, pointing.

Mina jumped up. "Ooh, a treasure chest! There could be *anything* in there: diamonds, gold, redstone. Should we look?"

Will felt a shiver of excitement. He nodded and hurried over. As Mina squatted beside the chest and lifted the creaky lid, he leaned forward and peered inside.

CHAPTER 4

"Ew!" The first thing Will spotted in the chest was a loaf of moldy bread.

Mina lifted the bread out with two fingertips and dropped it onto the ground. "Look, a velvet pouch!" she said, reaching for the sack that had been beneath the bread. As she shook it next to her ear, she smiled.

"Emeralds maybe?" she said hopefully. But as she poured the dark stones slowly into her palm, she scrunched up her nose. "Just seeds. Watermelon seeds."

"But wait, what's below that?" asked Will, catching the glimmer of something shiny. *Please let it be a diamond sword,* he chanted in his head. *Please let it be a diamond sword.*

It wasn't—but close. "A diamond pickaxe!" said Mina, lifting the heavy tool from the chest. "This could sure come in handy down here."

Will swallowed his disappointment as Mina admired the pickaxe. Then she spotted something else and nearly dropped the axe. "Is that what I think it is?" She dug down deep into the corner of the chest and pulled out . . .

"An old apple?" asked Will.

"Not just an apple," she explained slowly, her voice full of awe. "A *golden* apple. Don't you know how precious this is?"

Not as precious as a diamond sword, he wanted to say. But he clamped his mouth shut. The spark in Mina's eyes said she would have disagreed.

While Mina admired her apple, Will took another walk around camp, hoping to find treasure of his own. Judging by the old potatoes and moldy bread, he was pretty sure the mineshaft had been abandoned. *So it's ours for now,* he told himself.

Thunk! Will's foot hit something hard. He tripped forward and landed on the cold, smooth bars of a track. A *minecart* track.

Ignoring the pain in his bruised knee, Will hopped back up, searching for the cart. Now he could finally take his minecart ride! But where was it?

He followed the tracks to a large, iron door. No matter how hard he pressed and pulled on it, the door wouldn't budge. "How is a cart supposed to get through this thing?" he asked, leaning against the door with all his weight.

Mina looked up from the chest and cocked her head. "There must be a lever or button somewhere," she said.

Will slid his hand up and down the stone walls on

either side of the iron door. But try as he might, he couldn't find a switch. "The minecart tracks must go to the mines," he thought out loud. "Is there another way to get there?"

Mina stood up and brushed off her leggings. "Maybe through one of the tunnels?" she suggested.

"Good idea." Will was beside her in a flash, exploring the mouth of the nearest tunnel. "It's so dark," he said, straining his eyes to see.

Pop, pop, pop, pop, pop, pop, pop! Suddenly, the tunnel lit up with a long row of blazing torches.

"How . . . ?" Will was about to ask.

Then he saw Mina standing by the tunnel opening, her foot on an iron plate. She pointed down, a satisfied smile on her face.

"It's a pressure plate. Whoever mined down here was a redstone inventor!" she said, admiring the glowing red trail running from the floor to the first torch.

Will didn't have time to appreciate the mysterious miner's handiwork. Now that he could see his way along the tunnel, he was eager to find out where it led. He raced down the corridor almost as quickly as the redstone current itself.

"Will, slow down!" Mina called from behind.

But he didn't. He couldn't! He was sure that the minecart track was running alongside him, just on the other side of the wall.

The tunnel branched off several times, but the redstone torches lit the way. Will was getting closer to the heart of the mine now—he could feel it.

As he slowed down to turn a sharp corner, he felt something else: a blast of warm air coming from the cavern

at the end of the tunnel. A sign hung
just above the doorway.

Will read it and stopped dead in his
tracks.

CHAPTER 5

"What now?" Will asked Mina, who had finally caught up with him.

"We keep going," she said. "Just a little more carefully and a little more *slowly* this time." She was still breathing heavily from chasing after Will.

"So we head straight into the lava?" he asked. The heat coming through the doorway was already making him sweat.

"Well not *into* it," she said. "Just near it. There could be lots of great resources in there. Where you find lava, you sometimes find redstone and diamonds!"

Will shrugged and followed Mina into the cave. He could hear the bubbling, popping lava before he saw it. And the heat grew stronger. As they

came upon the glowing stream of red-hot lava, he pushed his sweaty bangs off his forehead.

"We sure don't need redstone torches in here," said Mina, taking in the orange glow of the lava on the cavern walls.

In the flickering light, Will could see across the hot lava stream to the other side. And what he saw there made his heart skip a beat.

"The minecart!" he said. "What's it doing all the way over there?"

Mina scratched her head. "Maybe there wasn't always a lava stream running through this cave. Sometimes when miners dig too quickly, lava strikes. It can fill a room in seconds!"

Will was only half listening. He had just spotted a stone bridge arching across the lava stream, and he wasted no time in jogging toward it.

"Be careful!" Mina pleaded.

But Will crossed the stones as quickly as he could. In the rising heat from the lava below, he felt like a melting candle. He had to get to that minecart. He'd been dreaming about riding one of them for so long!

The metal of the cart felt hot to his touch. He almost jumped in, but first, he had to figure out what powered this thing. Was there a coal engine? Will searched the carts before and behind. Nope.

Was it powered by redstone? Will examined the tracks for signs, like Mina would have. He saw torches placed beside the tracks, but they were turned off. Was the railway broken?

No. *There must be a button or pressure plate somewhere,* he told himself, just as there had been to light the torches in the tunnel.

He knelt to examine the track in front of the minecart.

There! A square iron plate rested in the middle of the next track. Was this the "on" button?

Will turned to ask Mina, but she was just stepping through an opening carved into the side of the glowing cavern. And out of that little cave came a giant "Whoop!"

Will jumped about a foot at the sound. "What is it?" he called to Mina.

One word echoed back: "Diamonds!"

Will took a step toward the bridge, and then looked back at the minecart. Did Mina have to find the diamond treasure right *now,* when he was about to set off on his minecart adventure?

He ducked down beside the minecart track and pretended like he hadn't heard her. If he could just activate the pressure plate, he could finally take that ride . . .

Mina's voice rang out again, louder than before. "Will, get in here! You won't believe this!"

He stood up with an exasperated sigh. It seemed like every time he found something amazing, Mina was pulling him back in the other direction. "It's not fair," he mumbled as he crossed back over the bridge, moving much more slowly this time.

Mina stood in the center of a small room, staring at a wall. Every other stone in that wall sparkled with whitish-blue flecks.

"I wish I'd brought my pickaxe," she said. "But *somebody* was in such a hurry to explore the tunnel that we left our pickaxes at the camp." She grinned at Will. "Let's walk back and get them!"

A seed of an idea grew in Will's stomach. "I have a better idea," he said. "Let's *ride* back and get them!"

Mina cocked her head. "The minecart, you mean?" She wrinkled her nose and shook her head. "No, that could be old and rickety. The track might split off or be broken in parts, and we could get lost—or even hurt. Let's walk back along the lit tunnel instead."

Will's chest was about to burst. He wanted to argue, but he couldn't. What Mina said made sense. He couldn't be sure that the tracks would lead safely back to camp.

But why do we always have to play it safe? he wanted to say. *And why do you get to decide what we do?*

He didn't say either of those things. He clamped his mouth shut and followed Mina along the tunnel, dragging his feet with every step.

CHAPTER 6

"What's wrong with you?" asked Mina. "Do you get grumpy when you're hungry?" She offered him a hunk of chicken from her lunch sack as they walked down the long tunnel.

"I'm not hungry," he mumbled.

"Well you should eat something if we're going to mine diamonds," she said. "It's a lot of work."

"I said, I'm not hungry," Will said again, louder this time.

Mina held up her hand. "Okay, okay," she said. "But remember what happened in the jungle when you didn't eat."

Why did she have to bring that up? He shuddered at the memory. He'd been so weak with hunger in the jungle that Mina had fed him a spider eye to restore his energy. He could still feel the slimy ball slipping down his throat.

He fought the urge to gag and then rummaged around in his pack for a piece of bread. He wasn't really hungry, but he didn't feel like arguing with Mina about it.

As soon as Mina finished her chicken, she started planning their mining expedition. "If we're mining diamonds," she chattered brightly, "the diamond pickaxe in that miner's chest will work better than our iron ones. Do you think he'll mind if we borrow it?"

Will shrugged. "How should I know?"

Mina shot him a look. "Really, Will?" she said. "We found diamonds today. The least you could do is be a little happy about it!"

But he couldn't be. Not when that minecart was sitting empty, waiting for a rider. Not when Mina was calling all the shots.

He quickened his pace down the lit tunnel, leaving Mina in his dust—that is, until he ran straight into a giant cobweb hanging from the ceiling.

"Gross! Get if off!" he hollered, trying to peel the sticky strands off his face. But the web was super strong. For a split second, he panicked, wondering what he'd do if a cave spider showed up right now. He'd be spider bait!

Mina burst out laughing. "Serves you right!" she said. "I should

leave you in there, since you've been acting like such a grump."

"Just get me out!" whined Will.

Mina giggled. "Hold still," she said, pulling the scissors from her pack. "If I cut the web carefully, we can use the strings for trip wire."

Will shook his head, or at least he tried to in the super sticky web. "Who are you going to set a trip wire for?" he asked. "There's no one down here except us!"

But no sooner had he said the words than they heard voices—loud voices, echoing down the hall.

"Shh!" said Mina. "Hold still." She quickly snipped a few strands of the spider web so that Will could push through.

He stood beside her, facing the voices, which were coming from the direction of base camp. *Is it the miner?* he wondered, feeling a wave of anxiety roll through his stomach.

A bobbing circle of light appeared on the wall at the end of the tunnel, growing bigger and brighter. Then three figures rounded the corner.

The first was a teenaged boy wearing a headlamp around his forehead. As soon as he saw Will and Mina, he smiled and waved. "Hello there!"

Will felt his muscles relax. This boy was too young to be the miner, and he seemed friendly enough. But the lanky girl with the dirty-blonde braid beside him wasn't smiling. Not at all.

And behind her? Will could just make out the hulking shape of a man. He wore a black eye patch, and he stared with his other eye—a cold, blank stare that made Will swallow hard.

Something was wrong. Mina must have felt it, too, because she grabbed

Will's hand. But she greeted the three strangers in her usual Mina-ish way.

"Is this your mine?" she asked brightly. "It's really well made. The redstone wiring is especially cool." She nodded toward the torches.

"It's our uncle's mine," said the boy, gesturing toward the man behind him. "But, hey, feel free to look around. Who knows? You might find a few *surprises*."

Is he telling us about the diamonds? wondered Will. That seemed strange. Why would a miner want to share a treasure like that?

He stepped aside to let the boy and girl pass. As the man with the eye patch pushed past, too, Will held his breath. *Don't look at him,* he thought, staring at the ground below. He swallowed another lump in his throat.

Finally, the strangers had disappeared down the tunnel, but Will and Mina stood perfectly still.

"That boy was lying," she said matter-of-factly. "This isn't his uncle's mine."

"How do you know?" whispered Will, hoping their voices wouldn't carry.

"Because all three of them had iron pickaxes strapped to their belts. Why would they use iron pickaxes and leave the diamond one back at camp?" she asked. "They stumbled onto this mine, just like we did."

Will was about to compliment Mina on her detective work. But suddenly he heard a *pop,* and everything went black.

"*Will?*"

"I'm here," he whispered. "What happened?"

"The power!" she said. "It went off. Or maybe it was *shut* off."

A chill ran down Will's spine. "Shut off?" he asked weakly.

"Yes!" Mina insisted. "That's why that boy was wearing a headlamp. They planned to leave us in the dark all along! Those treasure hunters don't want *us* finding the diamonds—that much I know."

As they fumbled forward in the dark, Will realized something, too. Without the torches to guide their way, they'd soon be lost in the maze of dark tunnels. And without the light of the torches, monsters would spawn. *Everywhere.*

"We're in trouble," he whispered. "That much *I* know."

CHAPTER 7

Will reached for Mina's arm in the darkness but felt nothing. "Mina?"

"Back here," she called, her voice echoing in the tunnel. "I have an idea."

Will heard the tinkling of glass bottles, and then Mina thrust one into his hand.

"Drink this," she ordered. "It's a potion of night vision."

Will hesitated. Ever since the spider eye incident, he'd been wary of anything Mina tried to give him. *But do you have a better idea?* he asked himself. *Nope.* So he raised the bottle to his lips.

The thick liquid tasted like carrot juice. *Ugh.* But as soon as he'd swallowed some, he could see the bottle in his hand. Orange liquid splashed at the bottom.

Then he could see Mina beside him, too, clear as day. "Cool!" he said, waving his other hand in front of his face. "I can see everything!"

"It won't last forever," Mina warned, zipping her pack back up.

"Let's try to find base camp. We can turn on the torches from there."

But even with night vision, Will and Mina couldn't figure out which way to go. With the torches turned off, every tunnel looked exactly the same, and one branched off the next. Will had the sinking feeling that they were walking around in circles.

Just as he was about to admit that, he heard a sound that made his stomach drop. It was the scuttle of spider legs—*lots* of them. *Uh-oh.* He drew his sword in a flash, ready for battle. But where were the spiders?

Mina whirled around too, searching for the monsters. "Where are they?"

Will looked one way
down the tunnel, then
the other. He searched for
holes in the rocks at his
feet—cave spiders were

small enough to squeeze through them.

Then he heard the sound again—
above him.

Will whipped his head upward
just as the hissing, red-eyed spider
dropped from the ceiling.

He swung his sword wildly and flung
the heavy creature away from him.
But others were coming, hissing and
squealing from the depths of the tunnels.

Will raced toward the sound,
hoping to catch the spiders off guard.

If he hit them at a sprint, he could knock them back. But Mina called after him. "Those are cave spiders!" she warned. "Their bite is deadly. Run *away* from them—fast. *Don't get bit.*"

Will stopped short and started backing away, just as the first spider scuttled around the corner. He swung his sword again and again as the red-eyed monster pushed him backward down the tunnel.

Other spiders dropped from the ceiling, and out of the corner of his eye, he saw Mina ducking and dodging them. But he couldn't take his eyes off the furry-legged beast in front of him. *Don't get bit,* he reminded himself.

The red-eyed spider lunged, and Will stepped back, swinging his sword. As they did their battle dance around another corner, Will felt a wave of heat at his back. That could only mean one thing: *lava*.

Now Will had the advantage, because he knew exactly where he was and what to do next.

He led the spider into the glowing cavern, where the monster seemed confused by the light. He took a step toward Will, then backward, and then sideways, his legs moving in all different directions.

Will poked the monster with his sword, trying to anger him. It worked!

The beast came alive again and lunged toward Will. Slowly, he lured the spider forward, closer to the bubbling lava, and then closer still.

With one wild swing, he knocked the spider into the red-hot stream. The monster sank with a long, slow *hissss*.

Exhausted, Will slumped to his knees. Then he heard a cry of pain from the dark tunnel beyond.

Mina.

CHAPTER 8

Will was at Mina's side in seconds. The spiders had cleared the tunnel, which was now lit with the glow from the lava stream. But Mina lay crumpled on the floor, tiny and pale. She whispered something to him.

"What?" He leaned closer.

"Milk."

Will dove into the stash of bottles in her pack, searching through colored potions to find anything that looked like milk. There, a full white bottle! He unscrewed the cap and lifted it to her mouth.

Some of it streamed down Mina's chin, but she managed to swallow a mouthful. As the color returned to her cheeks, she kept her eyes closed.

Will felt a wave of guilt. "I'm so sorry I left you behind," he whispered.

She smiled weakly. "It's okay. I guess I just wasn't as fast as you."

Will shrugged and glanced at the milk bottle in his hand. "You're a quick thinker, though," he said. "And your potions are pretty amazing, too."

As he tucked the bottle back inside Mina's pack, she propped herself up on an elbow. "Do I have any food left in there?"

Will dug deep into the pack. At the very bottom, his hand grasped something smooth and round. It was an apple. *No, not just an apple,* he corrected himself. *A golden apple.*

As he pressed it into Mina's hand, she smiled with relief. She took a big bite of the juicy fruit. When she opened her eyes again, they looked clear and bright.

"You know, you really should eat something too, Will," she said with a grin. "You look terrible."

He laughed out loud. Mina was back! And she was going to be okay.

Who needs a diamond sword? he thought, remembering how disappointed he had felt when Mina had opened the miner's chest. *Maybe that golden apple was the real treasure after all.*

He helped Mina to her feet and then leaned against the tunnel wall, looking in both directions. "Now what?"

"Well," she said, "we can't go back the way we came—not unless we want to visit our friends the cave spiders again."

"So this way?" asked Will, pointing toward the lava stream.

Mina nodded. "Maybe we can find another button or pressure plate in there to turn the torches back on."

But as soon as they stepped into the steamy hot cavern, Will heard voices. He grabbed Mina's arm and froze. "I think they're in the diamond cave," he whispered.

"So . . . we'll go the other way," she said, walking slowly backward as if she were fighting off a cave spider.

"Right," said Will. But when he tried to back up, he hit something solid—or *someone.*

The one-eyed man said nothing. He gripped Will with one hand and Mina with the other. Before Will could even think about reaching for his sword, the man had dragged them into the diamond cave.

This time, the teenaged boy seemed much less happy to see them. He lowered his pickaxe and nudged the girl at his side. She scowled too, but kept hacking at the diamond-flecked wall.

The boy took a step forward and narrowed his eyes. "Maybe you didn't hear me the first time," he said. "This is our mine. You're trespassing."

Will's mouth went dry, but chatty Mina had no trouble speaking.

"Actually," she said, "we were just leaving. If you could, um, turn on the lights for us, we'll be on our way." She plastered on a smile and turned to go, but the one-eyed man stood in her path. His hand reached for the handle of his sword.

Will's heart thumped wildly in his chest. *These treasure hunters won't actually hurt us, will they?* He chanced another look at the man's cold, dark face and had his answer.

Run! he wanted to scream at Mina. But where? He searched the walls of the cave looking for clues—anything that might help them survive.

The diamond-studded walls looked thicker than thick. But just above the area where the girl was mining, Will saw something: a thin, red crack. The longer he stared at it, the wider and brighter it became.

Then he heard it—the bubbling sound Mina had warned him about when they'd started exploring this ravine.

Lava.

CHAPTER 9

Mina saw the trickle of lava, too. She and Will locked eyes for a moment. But instead of warning the girl with the braid to stop mining, they stayed quiet.

One more *whack* was all it took. The stone crumbled, and a red-hot river roared into the chamber.

When the one-eyed man jumped backward in surprise, Will and Mina were ready. They sprang into action and raced past him.

"This way!" hollered Mina, veering left toward the dark tunnel that led back to camp.

Will shook his head. In a split second, he could imagine it all: even if they could find their way through the twisting tunnel, it would quickly fill with lava. They'd never be fast enough. But he had an idea.

"Follow me!" he said, sprinting toward the stone bridge that led to the minecart. He hoped that this time Mina would let him lead.

As he raced across the bridge, lava licked at his heels, but he kept going, toward the minecart toward the tracks that he hoped would carry them to safety.

When he heard Mina's footsteps behind him, he breathed a sigh of relief. "Get in," he ordered, whirling around to help her into the minecart.

"But where does it go?" she asked in a shaky voice. Her wide green eyes searched the shadowy tunnel ahead.

"I don't know, but sometimes you just have to leap in," said Will.

When she was sitting down safely, he grabbed the edge of the heavy cart and slowly pushed it forward. If he could just get it to roll onto the next piece of track . . . He gave one great heave, and the wheels squeaked forward.

Sure enough, as soon as the cart hit the iron pressure plate, the track ahead lit up. Glowing red rails stretched deep into the dark tunnel, with redstone torches placed every few feet along the track.

Mina gasped in surprise, but Will didn't have time to admire the lit tunnel. He couldn't waste another

second. He leaped into the cart and held on for dear life.

The cart lurched forward. Then it took off like a shot, flying down the rickety rails.

While Mina covered her face with her hands, Will looked over his shoulder at the cave they were leaving. Lava had already begun to pour onto the track behind them. *This is a one-way ride,* he realized. *There's no going back.*

"Will!" Mina shrieked.

As he whirled around to face forward, he saw the split in the track ahead.

"Which way?" she cried.

"I don't know!" he said. But even if he did, he didn't know how to control the cart. "Just hang on!"

Sparks flew as the cart veered sharply to the right, up an incline and back down again, and around another bend.

Will held his breath, hoping the track would lead them to camp and not back into the depths of the lava-filled mine. He kept his eyes trained on the tunnel ahead. And then he saw it: a dark mass where red tracks should have been.

"What's that?" he asked, pointing into the darkness. "Is that a door?"

Mina's jaw dropped, and she buried her face in her hands again. "I can't look!"

Sure enough, a heavy iron door blocked the path ahead.

And as the minecart barreled toward that door, it showed no signs of opening.

CHAPTER 10

As the cart raced toward the iron door, Will's eyes scanned the dark tunnel, searching for an escape route. *This was all my idea*, he knew. *And I put Mina in danger!*

Then his eyes spotted something shiny in the track ahead: an iron pressure plate. That could only be for one thing.

Will clung to the side of the cart and closed his eyes, making one last wish. *Please let it open the door.*

As the minecart zoomed over the pressure plate, Will heard a *creak*, and his eyes flung open. *Yes!* The giant door swung open just as the minecart reached the end of the tunnel.

In seconds, they had popped out of the darkness and back into the bright mineshaft. As the cart screeched to a halt, Will recognized the base camp. A wide-open room. Ladders to the world above. *Safety.*

His legs felt limp as he crawled out of the cart.

"Are you okay?" he asked Mina, whose face looked nearly as pale as it had after the spider bite.

She took a shaky breath. "I think so." She glanced back at the iron door. "That was sure a wild ride."

Will smiled. "Yeah. Even better than I thought it would be."

Mina punched his shoulder. "You *enjoyed* that? You're crazy."

Then her voice softened. "But you got us out of there, Will—faster than fast. How'd you know how to operate the cart?"

He shrugged, feeling heat rise to his cheeks. "I did what you do—I slowed down and looked for the signs. Kind of like in the diamond cave. You and I both saw that lava coming, but the treasure hunters sure didn't!" He paused and swallowed hard. "Do you think they made it out alive?"

Mina sighed. "I don't know. They seemed to know this mine better than we do. Maybe they found another way. I'm just sorry you didn't get your diamond sword, Will."

His hand gripped the handle of his iron sword. "That's okay. My iron one worked just fine against those cave spiders. But hey, you didn't get your slime!"

Mina fell silent beside him. When he turned to ask why, he found her staring at the minecart—or where the minecart used to be.

A giant green slime was sitting on the tracks instead.

Will sucked his breath in as the slime slid off the track and bounced toward them.

Mina was on her feet in seconds. She drew her sword and struck the slime, sending three or four smaller slimes bouncing toward Will. "Get the little ones first!" she called. "Or they'll surround us!"

Will drew his own sword and attacked the squishy, bouncing slimes. But each time he hit one, it exploded into smaller slimes. The gooey little mobs stuck to his legs, squished under his feet, and sprayed water until his pants were drenched.

But after a short, wet battle, he and Mina were finally staring down at a peaceful sea of green slimeballs. They lay perfectly still, like emeralds on the stone floor. Mina pulled out a sack and happily gathered them up.

Will thought about helping her, but the balls looked so *sticky*. He wiped his hands on his pants and said, "Now you can make your magma cream!"

Mina grinned. "That's not all," she said. "Watch this."

Using the miner's crafting table, she formed about nine of the slimeballs into a square slime block. "Help me with this," she grunted as she lifted the jiggly mass off the table.

Will helped her carry it to the floor, just beside the ladder.

"My turn first!" she announced, climbing the rungs. When she was about ten feet up, she stepped off the ladder and dropped to the slime block below.

Will cringed, but instead of the rough landing he was expecting, Mina bounced off the block and soared back up into the air.

"Whee!" she said. "This is fun!"

She bounced again, this time on her knees, and sailed back up. Her laughter

rang like chimes throughout the open mineshaft.

"It's like a trampoline!" said Will, amazed by Mina's invention. But he was even more amazed by how much fun she was having right now. *So Mina* does *know how to have fun,* he realized. *Once the hard work is done.*

After Will took a turn on the slime block and they had packed up their sacks, they climbed out of the mineshaft. The long ladder led to another ladder, and another, until they finally pushed open a wooden trapdoor and climbed out into the blinding light.

"Oh, sunshine!" exclaimed Mina, lying flat on her back and soaking up the rays. "I think we should explore the desert next. No more dark, damp caves."

But Will had spotted something in the distance: a jagged row of ice-capped mountains. "Or," he suggested, "we could head farther north. I've heard you can make crazy-fun snow slides on those icy slopes!"

Mina groaned. "I don't know how you do it, Will. You go straight from minecart rides to snow slides!"

"What?" he asked. "What's wrong with a little fun and adventure?"

She shaded her eyes. "Nothing's wrong with it—nothing at all." She sighed. "But you know, we're not always going to agree on what to do next."

Will thought of the lava-filled cavern below—of the adventure they'd just had together. "Maybe we won't," he said. "But we sure work well together when we need to."

Mina smiled warmly. "You're right. We really do." She hopped to her feet and pulled her messy hair back into a smooth ponytail. "So, should we get going?"

Will nodded. "We can make good time heading downhill."

Mina laughed as she started down the steep slope. "This time," she called over her shoulder, "watch your step!"